BiG MACHINES
Emergency! Emergency!

Amelia Marshall

WINDMILL
BOOKS

Published in 2017 by **Windmill Books**,
an Imprint of Rosen Publishing
29 East 21st Street, New York, NY 10010

Editor: Melanie Palmer
Designer & Illustrator: Dan Bramall
Design Manager: Peter Scoulding
Picture researcher: Diana Morris

Picture credits: ChameleonsEye/Shutterstock: 22-23; Dobresum/Shutterstock: 4bl, 14-15, 29r; Paul Drabot/
Shutterstock: 12-13; Flying Colours/Getty Images: front cover; Andrew Holt/Getty Images: 3, 5b, 8-9, 28br;
V S Luma/Shutterstock: 4cr, 26-27, 28cr; nicolamargaret/istockphoto: back cover, 24-25; Sue Robinson/
Shutterstock: 5c, 20-21, 29l; Shane Shaw/istockphoto: 4br, 6-7, 28bl; Twigra/Shutterstock: 10-11; VanderWolf
Images/Shutterstock: 16-17; Dmitry Vereschagin/Shutterstock: 18-19.

Cataloging-in-Publication Data

Names: Marshall, Amelia.
Title: Emergency! Emergency! / Amelia Marshall.
Description: New York : Windmill Books, 2016. | Series: Big machines | Includes index.
Identifiers: ISBN 9781508191926 (pbk.) | ISBN 9781508191896 (library bound) | ISBN 9781508191810 (6 pack)
Subjects: LCSH: Emergency vehicles--Juvenile fiction.
Classification: LCC PZ7.M377 Em 2016 | DDC [F]--dc23

Manufactured in the United States of America
CPSIA Compliance Information: Batch #BS16PK: For Further Information contact Rosen Publishing, New York, New York at 1-800-237-9932

Emergency! Emergency!

Written by Amelia Marshall
Illustrated by Dan Bramall

WINDMILL
BOOKS

Flashing lights and sirens wail –
NEE NAW! NEE NAW! NEE NAW!

The vehicles get ready with a **ROAR, ROAR, ROAR!**

Big, red fire engine with TURNING big, black tires, charging through the busy streets to put out all the fires.

Police car **SCREECHES**,
the sirens blare away.
EMERGENCY! EMERGENCY!
Make way! Make way!

Speedy police motorcycle
ZIPPING really fast,
ZIG-ZAG ZAGGING
with blue lights flashing past.

Quick! Quick!
The rescue plane
is RACING through
the sky,

climbing through the clouds, flying way up high!

Airport fire truck
is waiting on standby,
HEAVING
hefty water tanks
while all the
planes fly by.

Snow rescue vehicle **CHUGS** across the **snow**, pushing through the ice, **Hurry! Hurry! Go!**

Creak, creak, groan!
Rescue truck is ready.
HEAVE HO, HEAVE HO,
steady, steady, steady!

NEE NAW! NEE NAW!
Blue lights are FLASHING.
Hurry out of the way,
the ambulance is dashing.

Lifeguard van is on patrol **UP** and **down** the beach.

Driving over sand and surf,
no one is out of reach!

23

Lifeboat to the rescue!
CRASH! CRASH! CRASH!
Jumping over bumpy waves,

Splish! Splash! Splash!

Chugga! Chugga!
Chugga!
Big propellers chopping!
Helicopter hovers –
it rescues without stopping!

Now all is safe and all is calm,
the emergencies are done.

28

The sirens slowly stop their noise,
lights out now, one by ONE.

Emergency terms

Siren - loud sound to warn people to move out of the way.

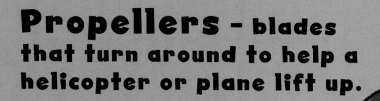

Propellers - blades that turn around to help a helicopter or plane lift up.

Ladder - helps firefighters to reach tall buildings.

Hose - a tube that carries water, used to fight fires.

Wings - help a plane to lift and fly.

Motor - machine that supplies power to a vehicle to make it move.

Crane - a machine that helps lift heavy loads.

Tires - cover wheels so they can grip the road.

For More Information

Archer, Mandy. *Fire Engine is Flashing.* New York: Scholastic, 2012.

Coppendale, Jean. *Fire Trucks and Rescue Vehicles.* Richmond Hill, ON: Firefly Books, 2010.

Dale, Penny. *Dinosaur Rescue!* London: Nosy Crow, 2015.

Reinhart, Matthew. *Rescue: Pop-Up Emergency Vehicles.* New York: Random House Children's Books, 2011.

For web resources related to the subject of this book, go to: www.windmillbooks.com/weblinks and select this book's title.